One LITTLE Kiss

ROBIN COVINGTON

Burning Up the Sheets, LLC
23139 Laurel Way
Hollywood, MD 20636

Visit my website at www.robincovingtonromance.com.
Edited by Nicole Bailey at Proof Before You Publish, Inc.
Cover design by Sweet & Spicy Designs.
Formatting by Anessa Books

Manufactured in the United States of America
First Edition May 2015

DEDICATION

For Debbie Hill Hodge and Tina Hobbs Payne.

Love you guys!

CHAPTER ONE

Leighton

The guy leaning on me really needs an Altoid.

I shift to the side as my impromptu airport floor roommate snuggles closer and lets loose a snore that makes my nearby fellow captives look in our direction in alarm. I'm not looking forward to riding out the snowstorm in Terminal D with a man who needs an industrial strength nasal strip but I fought hard for the prime spot along the wall close to an electrical outlet and I'm not moving.

When the airline had begun cancelling flights due to the unexpected blizzard three days before St. Patrick's Day, the first wave of activity in international departures was to secure a hotel room for the night. Being neither a platinum or some other precious gem level member at one of the big hotel chains had meant I was out of luck in securing any kind of room for the night so I'd wedged my way in between overstuffed carry-ons and whiny kids to grab my piece of prime real estate along the wall.

Two hours later, my phone is fully charged but the answer is clear—there is no room for me in the inn. Or the Marriott. Or the Hilton.

A great way to start my first adventure.

Two and a half months from my college graduation and I'm taking the chances in my life that I should have been taking all along. Finally. I'm beginning to feel like the person I am supposed to be but not everyone is on board with my accelerated program of development. The parentals, my twin brother—they mean well but they worry about me. Too much.

I am the fragile one. The one who needs to be careful. The one they almost lost. You'd think beating childhood leukemia would have made me brave, fierce. Nope. I'd bought into their characterization and worn it like a cloak to protect me from the big bad world until I'd almost suffocated under the weight. And then a few months ago, Brian-the-cheaterface had kicked my ass to the curb two weeks before Christmas for a girl named Silver who had green hair, ear gauges and a tongue stud and blamed it all on my being only slightly less boring than a bag of flour. Actually, his exact words were "if you'd only live with the passion you put into your fucking music I wouldn't have had to look elsewhere" but it all amounted to the same thing.

And as big a cheating asshole Brian was, he wasn't wrong.

So, I wallowed in my misery for a week and then grabbed the nearest bottle of champagne and proceeded to spend New Year's Eve "living with passion" in the bed of a guy I'd wanted for what seemed like forever. I also beat feet out of there before the morning after ruined the memories of the night. A cowardly move, I know.

He must have been on the same page because he avoided me in the weeks following our night of sweaty fun between the sheets. The times when we had to be together were infrequent but held a level of awkward somewhere between catching your parents making out on the couch and leaving the restroom with your skirt stuck in your panties. Good times.

But I am determined to live with passion, so when my music program selected me to go to the Celtic Music Festival in Dublin a month ago, I dusted off my passport, spared a moment to regret the terrible ID photo, and booked my ticket.

And now my flight is cancelled until the snowstorm passes, I'm stuck in the airport with a million other spring breakers, and my folks have lost their minds. It isn't like taking a spring break trip to Ireland is the height of danger but you'd think I was pledging to marry a death-row inmate or something, the way they are acting.

They finally stopped calling after I let their calls go to voicemail but they weren't shy about pulling out the big guns and so the next series of calls were from their not-so-secret weapon—my twin brother Landon.

I hit the screen and sigh, making sure a little bit of bitch is added to the overall tone of annoyance. "Landon. I'm going to Dublin. The flights will be back on tomorrow. Stop calling."

"Number Two." I bite back the urge to tell him for the eleventy billionth time to stop calling me that childhood nickname. I was three minutes behind him in arriving on this planet and he never lets me forget it. "Mom is shitting a brick because she thinks you're going to be murdered in your sleep by someone who wants your carry-on."

I glance at the small backpack at my feet. Yeah, I have the usual electronics in it —iPad, iPod—but the real treasure is in the hard case tucked close to my side. My violin, Wonder Woman, is inside and worth at least a year of tuition according to the insurance papers. She is my best friend, an extension of my body. My heart. We've been together since I was sixteen years old.

"If someone wants her they'll have to pry her out of my cold, dead hands."

He laughs. "And that is exactly what mom's having a cow about."

"Landon," I sigh.

"Number Two."

Did I mention how much I hate that nickname?

"I wish everyone would stop treating me like I am helpless or something. I'm not going to break or have a breakdown because I have to sleep at the airport."

"We worry about you," he says and then mumbles something to himself I can't make out.

"What? What did you say?"

"Look. I sent the cavalry," he rushes in and I let out a groan that catches the attention of several of my fellow strandees. I smile, trying to reassure them that I'm not the wacko they need to worry about as he keeps talking. "It was either this or mom was going to call airport security."

"She didn't." If she did I was going to die on the spot. Melt into a pile of embarrassed goo and be nothing but a dark stain on the disgusting industrial carpet.

"She *didn't* because I offered a compromise."

"What kind of compromise?" But I knew. I knew because I saw it walking towards me with a slow grin and six feet three inches of lanky, sexy, muscled body. I can't help the way my mouth drops open on a whispered, "oh my God" as I end the call. Hell, I'm glad I can still form a sentence at this point in time since the last person I want to see and the one person I'm desperate to have saunters towards me.

Jonas Sutton.

The guy I spent the night with on New Year's Eve and then ditched before the sun came up. My brother's roommate and best friend.

He stops right in front of me, forcing me to look up to see his face. He stares down at me, not missing a damn thing and barely hiding the smirk teasing at his lips.

"Who's your boyfriend?"

I glance at the dude still leaning against my shoulder and lightly shove him away. He sways in the opposite direction for a nanosecond but then falls back against me, a loud snuffly snore joining the waft of bad breath he aims in my direction. I shudder and try to breathe through my mouth.

Jonas shoves his hands in his pockets but I'm not fooled by the casual manner, the zinger is coming. He'll never let a moment like this pass him by.

"You gonna ditch him in the morning too?"

And there it is. I couldn't have done it better myself.

"You've been waiting since New Year's to say something like that, haven't you?" I ask.

"It seems appropriate considering the last time I saw you." He leaves the "since you've been avoiding me" unsaid and hanging in the air between us. I could point out that he has avoided me too but it's hard to point fingers when I am the one who started it with my "diddle and dash".

Jonas continues on with the business at hand. His apparent rescue mission. "I'm on the other side of the terminal and my flight to Rome was canceled too. My dad's assistant was able to grab me a hotel room about two blocks over from the airport and you're coming to stay with me."

Of course he has a room. The Suttons are rich from their furniture manufacturing business and they're probably super-platinum-kryptonite members at every hotel chain on the planet. There is no way Mr. Sutton is going to let Jonas sleep on the floor of the terminal.

But I can't go with him. It isn't that I don't want to go. The prospect of spending the night with Jonas is electrifying. My pulse kicks up to one hundred yard dash speed and I struggle to keep myself in check. I just *can't* go.

Jonas does it for me. Not just physically but he gets me right in the gut and the area dangerously close to my heart. I don't have room for him right now, everything already feels too big as I stretch to allow myself to grow. If I let him in, I don't know if I can breathe.

"Wow. Okay. That's really nice of you but I'm good right here." I pat the ground beside me and nudge the dude on my shoulder one more time. "I've got a good spot here on the wall."

Oh sweet baby Jesus. Can I just stop talking?

"I thought you'd say that." He pulls his phone out of his pocket and thumbs the screen, fingers tapping along on what I can only assume is a text. He stops typing and waits, looking at me with a completely unreadable expression on his face. I open my mouth to ask him if he is going to stand there all night when my phone vibrates in my pocket. I pull it out, key in my password and see that I have a text from Landon.

Great.

I swipe it open.

Go with him or mom will call the National Guard. You know I'm not kidding.

Fuck. Fuckity fuck. He is dead serious. I don't think for one minute that the National Guard will do anything if my mom calls them—I am sure they have a class in boot camp on how to blow off hysterical, overprotective parents—but she'll spend the night calling anybody. Everybody. She'll be insane and I'll be a horrible daughter for letting her worry when a solution is right in front of me.

I groan and dip my head in defeat, banging the phone against my forehead in the drumbeat of the defeated.

"I take it from your moment of melodrama that you've decided to go with me," Jonas breaks into my thoughts, his tone sarcastic and very sexy. Damn him. I look up, a glare plastered on my face with the fervent hope that he can't see the way my hands shake. "Let's go. We're going to have to walk and I want to get there before dark."

He reaches out a hand, leaning over to help me off the floor. I shove the snoring dude, trying to prop him up on the wall but not having much hope that he won't fall over in a heap the minute I'm gone. I snag my backpack and Wonder Woman and accept his assistance. My ass has gone to sleep from sitting on the barely padded floor and I'm grateful for his support because my legs are also tingly and weak. I stumble forward when I stand and fall into Jonas.

I'm tall at five feet nine inches so we touch everywhere. Thigh to thigh, chest to chest and the way he is leaning into my space our mouths are within inches of each other. My sensory memory recalls the smell of leather and cedar from his cologne, the whiff of the oil paints he uses, the sweetly clean smell of his fabric softener, and the underlying scent of Jonas that makes my mouth water.

He tastes as good as he looks and twice as good as he smells. I know this because I spent hours sampling every inch of him that night. The smooth silk of the skin on his shoulders, the rougher texture of the hair on his chest and legs, the surprisingly soft bristle of his goatee and the even softer feel of his lips.

I lick my lips, probably smearing my lipstick. But it is primal. I couldn't stop it if my life depended on it.

His gaze lingers on the place where my tongue has just been and I know in that instant that I'm not the only one struck with an inconvenient bout of lust right here in Terminal D. This is going to be a long night.

"I always did love how red looked on you," Jonas says, his voice catching a little bit on the last word. He pauses for the briefest second, as if he is memorizing the exact shade of red lipstick, before shaking his head and backing way. He rubs his jaw as a strange grin teases his lips. "C'mon Red. We need to get moving."

I follow after him, stupidly noting how good his ass looks in his well worn jeans. The good girl sitting on my right shoulder notes my objection to the idea of spending a night in a hotel with this man on her clipboard but I already know how this is going to turn out.

I only hope I can walk away again when the sun rises tomorrow morning.

CHAPTER TWO

Jonas

There is only one fucking bed.

I'm stuck for the night in a hotel room with Leighton and her goddamn red lipstick and there is only one bed. I dump my backpack on the floor and take the three steps necessary to grab the phone from the bedside table. I punch the button for the front desk, lower myself to the mattress, and wait for the clerk to pick it up. It rings once, twice, cutting off halfway through number three when she answers.

"How can I help you?"

"Can we have a cot delivered to room 1503?" I take a steadying breath, rubbing my sweaty palm against the denim of my jeans. My hands still shake when I automatically reach for my pack of cigarettes. Damn it. Two years past quitting and it is still a natural reflex.

"I'm sorry Mr. Sutton but we don't have any cots left."

"Well, can we get a room with two beds?" I silently plead with the universe not to fuck with me tonight. Not with this girl. I stood up and played white knight when Landon called me and surely that was enough to cut me a break?

"We don't have rooms vacant in the hotel."

Of course they don't.

My vision blurs in my right eye and I blink rapidly, rubbing it with my palm as I thank her and hang up the phone. My left eye is clear and my vision is as good as it could be in the dimly lit room, but the shadows are fuzzier in my right eye as I lower my hand and scan the room. I'm getting used to these moments, the panic as my eyes adjust is no longer as sharp in my chest but still, I lower myself to the bed and close my eyes.

I feel the bed jostle a little under Leighton's weight when she joins me, her sigh long and loud in the room. I don't need to look to know that she is close, her head mere inches from mine on the coverlet.

"So I guess we're sharing a bed," she observes. "I can be a big kid about it if you can."

I huff out a laugh of sorts at her words. A few months ago and I might have been quick to agree with her but after New Year's Eve, denying the feelings I have for Leighton is impossible. I'm not even touching her but the knowledge that she is so close, the smell of her rose perfume and the sharp metallic edge of the snow and cold on her hair puts me on edge.

"I promise to keep all my boy parts away from your girl parts," I say, trying to keep it light. I didn't miss the carnal equivalent to electroshock therapy that happened when we touched back at the terminal. I want this girl. I have always wanted this girl.

But once again our timing sucks.

She says nothing and I turn my head towards her, slowly opening my eyes to look at her. My vision is clearer or I'm closer than I thought because her big hazel eyes are staring right at me, her hair has fallen in a damp tousle around her face and those ruby red lips make my breath stutter audibly in my chest. Everything on me gets tight, even my chest is constricted, my cock getting hard under the cover of denim.

But I know the reason she left me naked and alone on New Year's morning. The same reason I didn't pursue her. I know where she lives. Fuck, I know where Landon keeps her spare apartment key at our place. She's not fuck buddy material, not even a casual girlfriend. Leighton—my Red— has "the one" written all over her.

What has pulsed between us for four years has always had the potential for the kind of greatness that can make you happy your whole life or bring you to your knees and never let you back up. We didn't have the space for that four years ago and we don't have it now. There's already too many moving parts in our lives.

Her stomach growling stops me from doing something outrageously stupid. Her eyes fly wide open, a flush of red creeping across her neck and cheeks just seconds before she covers her face with her hands. I laugh, not only because it's hilarious but from relief that the spell has been broken for a moment and I have another mission. I'm better when I have things to keep my hands busy.

Idle hands. Devil's workshop. I have a front row seat for that class.

"Let's find you some food." I lever off the bed and reach for my wallet and the room keys lying on the TV stand. "The hotel restaurant is closed but the desk clerk said there's a pub open around the corner."

Leighton hesitates at the edge of the bed, head dipped down, hair shielding her face from me.

"If you're worried about the snow, you've got sturdy boots on. We should be fine."

She shakes her head, auburn strands catching what little light is given by the bedside table lamp. I watch as Leighton leans down and grabs the case that holds her violin.

"It's not that. There's no room safe and I don't want to leave Wonder Woman."

"I'll carry it. No problem." I take the hard case from her and sling it over my shoulder as we leave the room and take the elevator down the fifteen floors to the lobby. The hotel is pretty quiet considering the number of people staying there. They must be exhausted after spending the day at the airport and are holed up in their rooms. The clerk nods as we leave and resumes her typing while the 24/7 news shows tell us there is a blizzard happening on every TV in the space. Thanks for the information, Captain Obvious.

Stepping out onto the cold sidewalk is like entering into another dimension and my fingers ache to hold a brush, a pencil. My sketchpad is in the room with my backpack but I know I'll try to recreate this scene later.

Everything is covered in white. The sky is a silvery, metallic gray only interrupted by the glistening flakes tumbling down in a constant fall of fat, fluffy snow. The blanket of two or three feet is a buffer against any noise and with the normal traffic off the busy street the hush is similar to the one found in a cathedral. The scenery is so clean, pristine, perfect. I hate to ruin it with footprints.

Leighton reads my mind. "I don't want to mess it up."

"I know." I look down a few blocks where I can see the warm glow of the pub's lights on the snow. "But food is down there."

She looks to where I'm nodding. "You can't just snap your fingers and put us over there?"

"I have magical powers but that isn't one of them."

Leighton slides a glance over to me and I see the heat. She's gone straight for the sexy in that innuendo. My dirty girl. It was the biggest surprise when we'd ended up in bed that night and I loved that about her. It didn't fit with the utter calm and poise she portrays to the world and I make believe that it is reserved only for me.

I shake my head. That kind of thinking has to end right here and right now or this night is going to end with me sleeping in the bathtub after a very cold shower.

"Let's go," I say and jerk my chin towards the lights.

She follows beside me and I extend my hand to steady her if she needs it. It isn't super slippery but you never know what is underneath the white stuff.

"So, are you still going to make the festival with this delay?" I ask as we switch from the uneven sidewalk to the obstruction-free middle of the road.

"Yeah. I'm not performing for a couple of days. I might not be as rested but I'll be there in time to perform." She glances up at the sky and then back at me. "Unless this becomes snowmageddon and we are stuck here until global warming cranks it up a notch or two."

"It's a big deal to be chosen for this festival?"

She dips her head but I see the flush embarrassment adds to the red already on her cheeks from the cold. "Yeah. It was an honor."

"And the job with the philharmonic after graduation? Second chair? Traveling all over the world?" Her head whips up in surprise and I shrug. "Your twin is the weakest link. He cannot keep a secret—especially when he's bragging about you."

"See? When you put it that way, I can't even be mad at him."

I laugh at her pout, grabbing her hand when I spy a suspicious looking patch of snow covered ice. Her fingers slide into mine as if they are a piece in a puzzle. I'm not a hand holder, that's girlfriend/boyfriend stuff and those have been few and far between in my dating life. I prefer to keep it casual, and lucky for me lots of college girls are okay with it.

But holding Leighton's hand under this big sky; just the two of us and the snow?

I could do this forever.

I take a deep breath to slow down my heart. It's racing because that's what she does to me and I wonder what I was smoking to think I could keep my hands off her for a whole night. When I touch her, all my reasons get fuzzy on the edges and I don't know if I can explain them to anyone if they ask. And then she brings it all back into focus.

"Are you ready for graduation?"

I send up a silent apology to Landon because apparently the fucker can keep a secret. He hasn't told her about what's going on with me.

"I'm not graduating." I swallow hard and let the whole truth spill out into the silent air. "I'm not coming back to school after spring break."

That stops her in her tracks and when she pulls up short, she slides a little bit on the snow. I adjust my grip on her to hold both of her arms and pull her in closer. Not quite full-body touching but enough to the point where I can feel the warm exhale of her breath on my face and the chill when it cools down.

"What? Why? You're at the top of the class."

She's right. I'm a good student. A double major in business and fine arts—a compromise with my dad to appease his need for an heir to the company and my passion. And the fact that I'm a few credits shy of a degree and not going to finish is probably going to give my dad a heart attack. I remember the arguments the last few months, the disappointment and fear in his eyes. He's a good father and he loves me but if I stay even just a few more weeks, I'll lose it.

Leighton is still waiting for an explanation and as I look down into her troubled gaze, all the reasons why I can't have her come back into sharp focus. And the irony of that thought and what I have to tell her hits me in the gut like a cheap shot in a barroom brawl.

"Leighton," I open my mouth and close it again, unable to process the words. I've faced this already, accepted it. But somehow when I tell her, it's gonna be real. "I'm going blind."

CHAPTER THREE

Leighton

My brain is frozen from the cold because I know I didn't hear him correctly.

"What?" I shake my head, as I'm giving him pointers on what his answer needs to be. "No."

"I'm sorry." He moves his hands from my arms to my face, stopping my movement. I'm still shaking my head in the negative, unable to stop. "Red. I thought you knew. Landon can't keep anything to himself. He tells you everything."

"He didn't," I halt and inhale deeply, steadying myself. "What *exactly* was Landon supposed to tell me?"

He stares at me, the muscle in his jaw pulsing with his irritation.

"I was diagnosed with retinitis pigmentosa just after Christmas. I got the final results on New Year's Eve."

Oh holy hell. The same day I'd shown up at his party, wallowing in my own heartbreak and toting a case of champagne. I'd been surprised when Jonas had reciprocated my interest, readily accepting my suggestion that we go to bed together. He'd been different that night. We'd both been unable to stay away from each other, to keep from touching each other.

I'd needed a touchstone. I'd needed Jonas to be my rock and apparently I'd been his as well.

"I don't understand. Can't they do something? Surgery? People get 20/20 all the time now. They do it in an hour."

I was babbling and he let me, his thumbs tracing a soft

pattern as he soothed me. *He* was going blind and he was doing everything to make *me* feel better about it.

"Red. They can't do anything. It's hereditary. You've met my grandfather."

I nod. Grandpa Sutton is blind and has been since his forties. He is debonair in that old-fashioned movie star kind of way, funny as hell, and had ably run the company for many years even after he'd lost his vision. I never thought of him with pity or worry because he is larger-than-life but this is Jonas. My Jonas. And I wanted to scream at the bad hand he'd been dealt.

Jonas is a painter. A wonderfully gifted artist that brings everything he sees to life in bright swaths of color and bold brushstrokes. His art is an extension of him. Vibrant. In-your-face. Clever. Flirtatious. Enticing.

The thought of him losing that gift causes my stomach to clench painfully. My chest aches with the tears I hold back, knowing he doesn't want to see them.

"How long?" He knows what I'm asking.

"It could be many years until I lose my sight entirely. Right now it gets fuzzy sometimes. Goes in and out. My peripheral vision is jacked up on occasion and I get headaches more frequently."

I can't stop the tear that runs down my cheek. It's scalding hot on my skin and then freezes. I squeeze my eyes shut, willing the rest of them back inside me.

Jonas groans and he wraps his arms around me, pulling me close to him. I loop my own around his waist and hold him tight, as if I can keep this burden away from him just by keeping him close.

"I'm not afraid, Red," he whispers into my hair. "I've watched my Grandpa and I know this isn't the end for me. My life will not be over. Just different." He brushes a kiss against my hair and sighs deeply, his voice pitching even lower. "I'll have a spot at the company, the support of my family. I'll be fine. I'll still be me. It's more than other people have."

I hear him. I know he's right but the unfairness of it all eats at me. Where is my shock? My numbness before the pain sets in? I am immediately in agony for him and struggling to keep my shit together. He's being movie-of-the-week stoic and brave and I'm on the verge of blubbering.

"I'm sorry you found out this way. I was sure Landon " He breaks off his thought, rubbing his cheek against my hair and holding me tighter. "I'm just sorry."

He's the one going blind and he's apologizing for how I found out?

I pull back to look him in the eyes, to see if I can gauge what level of bullshit he is shoveling at me. His coffee bean-colored eyes are clear, sincere, as they stare back into mine. I wonder how long it would be before this simple act of looking at each other would be impossible. The day when I look at him and he won't see me? It cuts me. Down to the quick.

I feel like I'm losing something I didn't even know I had.

"Don't apologize to me Jonas Sutton." I stop when I hear the anger in my tone. I considered reining it in but I just can't pretend. It isn't in me anymore. After the dumping by the cheaterface, I can't drown my own emotions anymore. Not when they are this important. I let my voice carry into the quiet, loud with my emotion. "This sucks and you're being gallant and brave and so goddamn calm about this whole thing!"

And then they began in earnest. Hot tears. I couldn't have stopped them if I tried.

Jonas stares at me, his own expression twisting into one of concern and pain. I suck in a deep breath, trying to calm down, knowing I am making him feel worse.

"Jonas." It's the only word I can form coherently at that moment but every ounce of what I am feeling is levied on those two little syllables. He reacts, hands moving again to cup my face as he leans in and takes my mouth in a kiss more compassionate than carnal.

It is warm, wet, and soft. Our tongues touch tentatively, cautiously. This isn't about sex; it's something deeper. It's us—Jonas and Leighton. We began this dance with one little kiss at the first freshman mixer in a dark corner of the deck of the student union. I was "Red" that night, long before he knew my last name. Before he knew I was the sister of his roommate. Before he knew about the leukemia. I wasn't ready for what bloomed between us then and neither was he. Now? I don't know but it doesn't scare me anymore. Well, it does. But only in the good way.

I'm not sure if I can expand to accommodate what Jonas would bring to my life with his energy, his vivacity, his joy. I've lived a half-life up until this point, tip-toeing around like the cancer would come back if I lived too large. But I am moving on, opening up and embracing my gift of being cancer free. That's what this trip is about and the job with the philharmonic.

Me. Living large. Finally.

One of us moans, low and deep and the kiss flashes hotter for a moment. Teeth clash as he dives in deeper and I grab his jacket and pull him closer. But just that fast it is over. Jonas slides his mouth over my cheek until he can whisper in my ear.

"I'm not brave. I'm not gallant. I'm not calm. I just can't change it."

We stand there for a few moments, the snow covering us with its cocoon of white. With the street deserted it's like we are the only two people in the world. There's nobody around to hear me but I whisper anyway.

"What are you going to do?"

"I'm going to travel and see the places I want to paint while I still can." He shudders out a breath and a laugh as he pulls away, wiping at his face. Snow or tears, I can't tell. "My dad is freaking out but my Grandpa intervened. I just can't sit in class and act like I don't have this countdown clock over my head. The doctors say it's usually years before I lose all my vision but each second feels like one that is wasted."

"I get that," I say, brushing the wetness off my own cheeks, hoping I don't look like I've been bawling in the street. When I look at him I smile as much as I can. He is doing exactly what I would do, what I *did* through all those hospital visits and treatments. It's always easier to be brave for other people. I wasn't going to bring him down but one thing needed to be said. Just so he would know. "I'll miss you."

He smiles back, tossing me the one where he only quirks up the right side of his mouth. It's sexy as hell and he knows it. It's his "got the world by the balls" grin and it's totally Jonas.

"Of course you will, Red. I'll miss you too."

He reaches out for my hand and leads me over the last of the distance to the pub. The noise from inside spills out onto the street even through the closed door. The rumble is loud and as Jonas tugs the handle next to a sign that reads "Flanagan's Pub", it reaches epic proportions, a wave of laughter and clinking glasses.

We get inside and it's packed to the gills, probably in violation of the fire code.

"Oh shit. That smells so good," Jonas says.

And he is so friggin' right. It is heaven. Really. This is what the hereafter should smell like. "I hope they have room for us because if I don't eat soon, I might become a cannibal."

"I'm going to pass on the obvious joke there."

I realize what I said and what he meant and while it was hilarious it brings back an altogether different kind of memory. In fact, my belly tightens as I remember being on my knees, his cock in my mouth. I'd loved it. The power to get him off. His pure enjoyment in the act. The sounds he made. The sting of his fingers clenched in my hair. The way he wanted to keep eye contact the whole time. Now, *that* was heaven.

I am saved from having to figure out something to say by a large, red-haired man approaching us with a big smile on his face.

"I'm Ryan Flanagan the owner. We've got two seats if you don't mind sharing a table."

Jonas flicks a glance in my direction and I nod in agreement. "Works for us."

"Follow me."

Jonas continues to hold my hand as we make our way in between the crowded tables. Everyone smiles at us as we pass, brothers and sisters in arms as we endure the plight of the stranded. And the beer flowing freely doesn't hurt either.

Ryan points to two seats on one side of a table in the middle of the pub, across from two guys who look to be in their early thirties. Both handsome, smiling and holding almost empty pint glasses. Quick introductions all around as we take off our coats and we learn that they are Peter and Gabe Scott, newlyweds, and on their way to the warmth of Key West for their honeymoon.

Ryan brings us up to speed. "Taps are open but the kitchen is limited. We've got stew or chili with homemade bread. When I saw how many people we'd have to feed I went for warm and filling instead of a full menu."

"A beer and stew for me," I say and Jonas signals for two.

"Coming up," Ryan says and then pauses, looking at the hard case Jonas is draping over the back of his chair. "You play?"

"She does," Jonas points at me. "Like an angel."

"You know anything Irish?" Ryan asks.

I open my mouth to respond but "Quick Draw Sutton" beats me to it yet again. "She's going to the Celtic Music Festival in Dublin to perform by invitation."

"If you want to play a couple of songs, just hop up there." He nods towards a smallish stage to the right and then heads back to the kitchen.

"You're a musician?" Gabe asks, leaning forward in interest. His hand is clasped with his husbands on top of the table and I realize that I miss the feel of Jonas' fingers intertwined with mine. We're sitting close and I can feel his warmth in the places where our bodies touch from shoulder, to hip, to thigh and knee. I lean into him and he nudges back.

"Yes. I am." I start to tell him that I'm just a student but then I remember the contract I signed two weeks ago with the symphony. "I'm actually the second seat violin with the Alkan Philharmonic or I will be after I graduate in May."

"That's amazing," Gabe says, his face lighting up like the music fan I suspect he is. "I saw them twice last year. I'd love to get season tickets one day."

"The next time you make it to a performance, come see me backstage," I offer with a smile. Excitement about the job zings through me and I fight the urge to open my email and look at the letter offering me the position again. I still expect them to take it back and will probably feel that way until my ass is actually in the seat at the first rehearsal.

Conversation stops when Ryan brings our food and drinks. For a few moments, we are silent as we tuck into our meal, our tablemates looking at us with barely disguised laughter.

"We were hungry," Jonas says in apology for our terrible manners and takes a sip from his pint. "Lunch was a long ass time ago."

"You'll be traveling a lot with the Alkan group," Peter says, bringing the conversation back to my new job.

I nod and can't help the grin that takes over my face. "I know. But I'd be lying if I didn't say it doesn't scare me a little. But this trip is my dry run. I've reserved a car and plan to just drive around a few days. Let the road and the music tell me where to go."

I've never done anything like this before and it is exciting and terrifying. Freeing.

"You aren't well-traveled?" Peter inquires.

"No. Not at all really." I grab my pint and take a sip before continuing. "I was very sick for a few years. When we weren't off to see a specialist we stayed close to home, close to my medical team."

I think back on those years. The somber drives to the appointments and the even darker ones on the return home. Vacations were taken but all under the unspoken umbrella that it might be the last time.

"You're okay now?" Gabe asks, bringing me back to the pub and the conversation.

"Yes. Six years in remission and doing fine." I turn and catch Jonas' eye and I see he is already watching me, his smile tender and sad. This is one night of fucked up revelations and I lean into him and feel his left hand under the table, lightly brushing against my thigh. Silent encouragement, a connection, and so much more. "I'm ready for the next adventure."

Gabe and Peter nod, thinking I'm just talking about the trip but I'm not. I tear my gaze away from Jonas because I don't want him to see what crazy shit is pinging around in my head right now. I think back to his revelation in the street and the grief that surges up from my soul makes my hand shake as I lift my glass to my lips once more.

I've spent four years telling myself that this thing with Jonas is the product of an overly romanticized night involving a girl away from home for the first time and a sweet, sexy, smooth-talking boy who made her feel desirable every time he called her "Red". But I think I might be wrong.

I am Red.

His Red.

And I love him.

All the time I wasted with Brian was marking time, passing time with someone who was safe and acceptable and fit in the box I put him in. It's no wonder he moved on to somebody who really wanted him and left behind the role of understudy to the lead actor in my little life drama.

Yes. I was devastated when he broke it off with me but I figured out a while ago that it was all ego. I stung with the hurt of him finally figuring me out and calling me on it. And who was the person I ran to?

Jonas.

I hadn't given it a second thought at the time but I've done a lot of second-guessing since then because I didn't want to think about what it really meant. And I don't know if it's the fact that he's going blind or the fact that I'm finally getting up the nerve to live, but I want my future to include the man sitting beside me.

But I can't forget the fact that he's avoided me since our night together. He's figuring shit out in his head. I get it, I really do. Learning that your body is not something you can control and it can turn on you at a moment's notice plays serious fuckery with your brain.

So, I do what I always do when the floor falls out from under me and I need something to help me land safely.

I grab Wonder Woman, walk to the little platform and start to play.

CHAPTER FOUR

Jonas

She's killing me.

Seriously. Every note of the song she plays is cutting in deep. I know she's upset, the news I delivered was hard for her to take because she cares. Leighton and I have always existed in this "Will they? Won't they?" alternative universe but we're friends and my illness will impact her deeply. But I also saw the look she laid on me before she stood up to play and I remember the kiss out on the street and suddenly everything is really complicated.

The pub is silent, only the rattle of dishes and the low-level murmurings of the wait staff as they continue to serve the crowd. Leighton is standing on the tiny stage, eyes closed, her bow moving in a gorgeous sweep across the strings as she brings the notes to living, breathing, shimmering life. I've painted her like this before. That space where she exists when she's performing is golden hued and warm. Nothing can touch her there and she is breathtakingly beautiful.

I have at least a dozen canvases to prove it.

"Your girlfriend is brilliant," Gabe whispers as he leans across the table. "I've never heard anyone play like that."

"She's played since she was three or four years old. She's on a full music scholarship at school." I pause and then correct him. "She's not my girlfriend."

I ignore the pang in my chest when I say the words out loud.

"Really? I just thought..." Gabe lets his words fade into

the music as he settles back in his chair.

The plaintive tune is sad and deep and aching with every drop of her emotions and I know she's playing for me even before our gazes meet across the room. I shiver, the sensation flashing down my spine, my arms, along my scalp. Leighton sways, stuttering a note and I realize she feels it too. Fuck. This is nuts. I won't survive the night at this rate.

She ends on a sweetly singular note that seems to stretch into the stillness until it fades away on an echo. The crowd is silent, suspended with the last fragments of the sound and then they blow up in applause. She breaks eye contact with me to smile at her audience, dipping her head in thanks as they add a few wolf whistles to the clamor. She laughs and tosses back her fall of auburn hair, lifts Wonder Woman to her shoulder and stomps out a heavy, quick beat on the floor before launching into a lively Celtic song made for a pub crowd.

I exhale the breath I was holding and shake it off. Grabbing the fresh beer Ryan has placed on the table, I take a long swallow, hoping the alcohol will take the edge off.

"The first time Peter looked at me like that, I ran," Gabe says, exchanging a rueful smile with his husband.

"I did not follow him," Peter adds. "But I did the next time. And the next."

"It's complicated," I say, unable to find a word to describe it better. I was not an English major.

"It always is when it's intense," Peter observes.

I stare at them, wondering just how much of my crap they want to hear. Fuck it. This night is already beyond weird. I can't talk to Landon about this. She's his sister. I might as well unload my life on complete strangers.

"I'm going blind," I begin, adding quickly when they look alarmed and begin to murmur words of condolence. I wave them off. "It sucks and it is a game changer for me. Flipped my whole future upside down. But I'm okay right now."

I know I sound borderline flippant but I'm not. My life

has been upended by this fuckery and I'm waiting for the anvil of grief, anger, and everything else to hit me and drill me into the ground. But for right now, I'm keeping my shit together. One minute at a time.

"Does she know?" Gabe inquires.

I nod. "I told her just before we came in here. I thought her twin—my best friend— told her but for once in his life he kept a secret."

"How'd she take it?" Peter asks.

"She was Leighton," I shrug, processing all the stuff mashing up in my brain. I try to explain this complex, smart, strong, and kind woman to them. "She was really sick like she said. It was leukemia and her family freaked out as anyone would. They started to think she was weak, fragile, but she's the strongest of all of them. She isn't brash or in-your-face about it. Leighton has this core of steel. She's solid. Nothing can move her from what she knows is right or wants to do."

Gabe says, "It sounds like she's the perfect woman to be with you as you deal with everything."

I nod. He couldn't be more right or wrong.

"She'd be great, my rock. I know it."

"But…?"

I inhale deeply, diving in to scoop out the worst of it and throw it on the table in front of these guys who probably realize that they have gotten stuck with the crazy.

"I'm so fucked in the head right now I don't even know what I want to do with this mess." I lay it all out there methodically, the business side of my brain kicking in to help me put it all in the right box. "I'm leaving school two months before graduation to travel, paint, and take some time to figure it out. I have no idea where I'm coming out at the end or when I'm coming back. I just know I need to keep moving at this point." I run my hands over my face, fatigue seeping out of my pores. It has been a long ass day. "She's got this opportunity with the philharmonic." I turn to look at her playing her heart out and I choke down the emotion that is rolling in my stomach. "Listen to her. She's got a goddamn gift and I will not get in the way of it."

"I'm assuming you haven't talked about any of this with her?" Gabe asks, continuing when I shake my head.

He turns to Peter and whatever passes between them is bittersweet and very precious. When he looks back at me, his expression is calm, peaceful. A sharp stab of jealousy hits me right over the heart. I haven't had that since I got the diagnosis, except for the few hours spent in bed with Leighton.

"I wasn't out when I met Peter. I knew my family would not be supportive, that I would lose them if they knew. How did you put it?" Gabe cocks his head at me and smiles. "Oh yeah...fucked in the head. That was me. Totally fucked in the head."

"He was a gorgeous mess and I didn't care," Peter adds, reaching out to take Gabe's hand. "He fought me every step of the way. He broke up with me. We got back together. I left him when I got tired of being in the closet with him. It was a roller coaster ride and not the fun kind."

Gabe jumps back in. "I know it isn't the same as what you are going through, but at the time it felt like I was going to lose a limb, something vital, if I had to watch my family walk away from me. No more Christmases, no more family vacations to the beach. There would be a lifetime of family photos without me in them. Those memories would never happen. It killed me." He took a deep breath, letting out the shakes that had taken over the last few lines. "I also knew Peter was it for me, just as essential. I couldn't breathe when he wasn't with me. It was really hard."

"So what happened? I assume you came out because you got married. Did your family come around?" I ask.

He shakes his head, bone deep sadness diluting the joy in his expression. "No, they didn't. The worst happened and I lost them."

"Shit. I'm sorry." And I was but I couldn't stop myself from asking. "So what changed your mind? What made you take the leap?"

They look at each other and I once again feel like I'm interrupting something special, a voyeur to a private moment.

Gabe speaks, never taking his eyes off Peter. "I thought of all those moments. Snapshots in my mind. Memories. *He* wouldn't be in them and that felt wrong down to my soul. I knew I would look back over my life and I'd know that something was missing. I would never have a complete picture. My life would never be whole and those memories, without him in them, would be meaningless."

"So he asked me to marry him," Peter added, his grin growing with every word. "Turned up at my office three months after our final breakup and got down on one knee with the ring and I said yes."

"Best. Memory. Ever," Gabe said and leaned over for a kiss.

I watched them have their moment. It was impossible for me to look away. I'd have to be a clueless asshole to not understand their message. Did I want to lose Leighton and all those potential memories? My heart said no, pounding in my chest like a drum. My head said that I didn't even know what was going to happen to me and that I couldn't drag her into the unknown like that. The scared part of me wanted to cling to her and hold on tight. It was a selfish impulse and I would not act on it. Not when she had all this good stuff ahead of her.

I am not that guy.

Leighton finishes playing and steps down from the platform, slowly making her way to the table as best she can with all the people shaking her hand and cheering her on. She glows—cheesy but true—the music lighting her up from the inside. Auburn hair, cheeks pinked with her exertion and those damn fire engine red lips create a picture that I cannot tear my eyes away from. I take a mental photo of this moment, not just to paint later but to file away for when the darkness descends.

Peter and Gabe leap up when she gets to the table.

"You were amazing!"

"Thanks," she says, looking over to me as she put Wonder Woman away in her case. "You okay?"

I nod. "Great. You were wonderful as usual."

She blushes, dipping her head and smiling wider at my compliment. I cannot help but smile back, enjoying her happiness in this moment.

Ryan rushes over to the table, pushing a paper bag covered item into her hands just as she gets her violin tucked away.

"Payment for your services," he says and plops down four shot glasses on the table. "You were fantastic. Come back anytime!"

She peeks into the bag and gives a little yelp of delight, pulling out the half size bottle of Jameson whiskey and showing it around.

"Anybody care to join me?"

We all agree, not crazy enough to turn it down. We sit while she opens the bottle and pours each of us a double.

"Are you trying to kill us?" Peter laughs.

"You're a big boy." She raises her glass and gives a salute. "To snowstorms and cancelled flights."

We all join her and she pours another round that ends with Gabe lifting his glass. "To memories worth keeping."

He looks at me when we drink and I don't know whether to laugh or pour another shot.

Leighton slides a glance between us, places her shot glass down with a thud on the table, and reaches for her coat.

"Jonas you grab Wonder Woman and I'll take the booze."

"We're going?" I ask, surprised. I don't have an objection to it but I figured she'd want to stay.

"If we finish off the bottle tonight, I want to be in the hotel," she says and quickly passes hugs, kisses and email addresses to Peter and Gabe.

"Congratulations," I say as I shake Gabe's hand goodbye.

"It's not easy but it's worth it." He glances over to

Leighton and then looks back to me. "She's strong. You said it yourself."

I nod, not knowing how to answer without starting a conversation that Leighton will want to join. I'm not ready to talk to her about it yet.

"Come on sailor," she jokes as she leads me out of the pub, her hand clasped in mine once again. I hang on like she's my lifeline and let her lead me straight into temptation or deliverance. Either one will do.

We hit the street and the winter wonderland hasn't changed except that the snow is deeper. Drifts are piling up against the buildings and the curbs and sidewalks have disappeared. The way back to the hotel will be tricky with no clue about what is underneath the pile of white so I lead her to the middle of the deserted street once again.

"I feel a little stoned," she says. I raise an eyebrow at that one.

"You only had a beer and two shots."

"It's the music. Pure endorphins. It's better than any drug. I get so amped up when I play I could stay up all night." She throws her head back, welcoming the fall of the flakes on her face. "Second star on the right and on until morning."

I laugh. She's quoting her favorite play, "Peter Pan". She must be flying.

"You were amazing. As usual." I am mesmerized by the way the glistening snow lands on her lipstick, shimmers for a moment and then dissolves into the blood red of her lips. I want to lean over and lick them off. She would taste like whiskey, and winter cold, and Leighton.

She smiles and pulls her hand out of mine, skipping ahead a couple of steps before lying down on the snow and making a snow angel. Her arms and legs make a wide pattern and I notice that she still has the bottle of whiskey in her hand.

"A drunk snow angel?" I joke. "Bad girl."

"Hey, even the angels have to sin at some point. Otherwise they never get to repent." She stops her movement, lying there with snow quickly covering her coat and clothes, smiling like she's on a beach in Tahiti. Crazy girl.

I could stare at her forever.

I extend my hand to her. "Get up evil angel. You're going to freeze."

She takes my hand and stands, shaking off the snow like a puppy and I can't help but laugh. What she says next, and the sexy way she says it, wipes the smile off my face.

"I know you'll warm me up." Leighton lifts up the small distance necessary to make up for our height difference and kisses me. Neither one of us closes our eyes as our lips brush against each other. It should be too sweet to get me going but my dick hardens in my jeans and I strain to resist the urge to drag her even closer.

Leighton breaks off the kiss but does not move away. Her eyes are dark, pupils wider with her arousal. I lick my lips. Just like I thought: whiskey, winter, and her.

"Red, what's going on?"

"Let's get drunk and tell each other everything we're afraid to say sober."

I choke, something between a laugh and something far more emotional tangling in my throat. She's quoting me. It was the dicktastic line I laid on her the first night we met four years ago.

"How could you stand me that night?" I ask.

"I thought you were hot," she says and we both chuckle before her expression morphs back into longing and I'm lost. "Let's be those kids. Let it end the way it should have that first night. My brother isn't your roommate and he doesn't scare you off."

Off limits. That's what Landon had said when he saw me kiss her. He told me she was fragile, that I needed to be careful with her. But she wasn't weak. She was strong but living for other people, protecting them with her caution. They didn't realize the difference or the sacrifice. The only thing she didn't compromise was her music.

The girl with the music was the one who rocked my bed as the year ended. I want that girl. I want to be the guy she met that first night. I want the thing that began with one little kiss and had such promise. If only for one night—I want it.

I take off a glove and raise my hand to trace a fingertip along her jaw.

"Your hand will freeze," she protests as the same time she leans into my caress.

"I don't care. I have to touch you."

I dive into her mouth, taking possession quickly, desperately and she opens to me on a hungry groan. Her tongue duels with mine for domination as she digs her fingers into my coat and drags me closer. The thud of the whiskey bottle slipping out of her hand and landing in the snow is not enough to make me stop. I cup her head, angling her lips as I take it deeper one more time before I break it off. I'm panting, out of breath but she finds a way to speak.

"You " she gulps in air, biting her lip, " you've got my lipstick on your mouth."

That flips every switch I have. I cannot stand to let her go. I need her. And even though I know this changes nothing in the long run, my decision is made for tonight.

"I want to kiss you again and smudge all your lipstick. I want to see it ring my cock when you suck me off and I want it to stain my skin and the sheets as I drown myself in you." I use both hands to cup her face and she gasps. "I'm all kinds of fucked up in my head. I don't know what I'm going to do or where I'm going to be. I don't really know anything anymore except that you look like a goddam angel and instead of letting you go the only thing I can think of is how much I want to take you back to our room, strip off your halo and watch you sin."

CHAPTER FIVE

Leighton

Jonas. Get the damn door open."

He grunts against the kiss I plant on his mouth as he fumbles with the key card again. It's only been a few moments since he blew me away with the speech on the street but it feels like an eternity and a half. I want him. My skin is tight with it and I feel like I'm going to combust if I can't get him inside me as soon as possible.

"You realize…" he mumbles against my mouth as he angles his head to get a better look at the lock on the door, "…that it is almost impossible to do anything with your hands on me?"

"You need to learn to work under distracting conditions," I say, letting my hands wander under the layers of his coat and Henley to map the smooth, hot expanse of skin on his abdomen. He grabs me tight around the waist and keeps me from diving back in for another lip lock while he finally gets the key in the lock and swings our door open.

"Holy fuck. You're going to kill me," he says as he drags me inside the room and uses the weight of our bodies to close the door as he pins me to it. He does not hesitate, diving in to run his tongue along the exposed column of my neck. Jonas tastes, sucks, bites and I shiver in spite of the abundance of clothing I have on and my only thought is to remove all of it as quickly as possible.

"Off," I demand as I tug at the zipper on his leather jacket, dragging it down his arms until it gets stuck on his elbows.

Jonas steps back and we both decide to tackle our own clothing because there is no time for slow, seductive stripper pole performances tonight. Our need is high, so hot there is a whiff of a lighted match in the air. Jackets, sweaters, boots, socks, jeans fly in every direction as we try to set a record for how fast we can get naked. I'm about to remove my panties, thumbs tucked over the waistband when Jonas stops me with two words.

"Christ, Red."

Even if I couldn't see his face in the one meager lamp we left on, the anguished tone of his voice tells me everything I need to know. I pause, dropping my hands as I let him get his fill.

"I want to paint you. Just like this." He steps forward, his fingers tracing the line of my collarbone with the whisper touch of butterfly wings. I'm electrified, nipples tight and sex wet as I relax into his touch, giving myself up to the pleasure.

He takes his time, exploring me with his touch and memorizing me with his eyes. I lift my hands, weaving my fingers into the dark waves of his hair, not directing his movement but anchoring myself to him as I feel my body begin to shake with my own desire.

Jonas dips lower, tracing the path in between my breasts as he lowers himself to kneel in front of me. I watch him, eyes intent as he explores me like I'm something precious. I find myself offering up a quick prayer that if I remember only one thing my entire life it is the expression of awe and desire on his face at this very minute. Every girl should feel like this at least once in her life.

"I have to taste." Jonas leans in, his lips soft and moist as he follows the curve of my right breast, nuzzling my flesh until the hint of teasing slides into the wet, white hot sensation of his tongue swirling my aching nipple. I remove a hand from his hair to brace it against the hotel room wall as my knees go weak with the decadent pleasure.

Jonas takes my reaction as the signal to devour me. One

nipple, then the other is sucked inside, flicked with the tip of his tongue, teased and caressed with his fingers. I'm babbling, words I'm not even sure exist in the dictionary because I can't think beyond processing the electrical signals of bliss zinging to my brain.

I protest weakly when he leaves my breasts and travels lower, large hands anchored on my hips, the fingers digging into my flesh with a grip that I'm sure will leave a bruise. I want the marks, the thought of them staying with me when I leave him tomorrow comforting.

He teases my flesh with soft kisses against my belly, the hair of his goatee adding a roughness that abrades my skin and sends tingles shooting out from the contact site. I know where he is heading and the anticipation is making me pant with my own desire, my fingers aching where they try to find purchase on the wall. My legs tremble beneath me, spreading involuntarily when I feel the warmth of his breath against the fabric of my panties.

Jonas stops, only the pressure of his mouth against my mound and I get wetter, my body begging him to take what I have to offer.

"My mouth is watering Red. I want to eat you up," he groans, the vibration against my clit making me whimper. "I'm going to peel back these panties and lick you until you scream. I want you to come hard and come fast. I need you to be very wet for how hard I'm going to fuck you. Do you understand?"

He lifts his eyes, hot and dark in the muted light of the room but I swear I see fire in them.

"Do it."

It isn't a plea. I don't have the patience to wait or the self-control to play games. I'll sign up for anything he wants to ensure that he puts his mouth on me in the next five seconds.

As I watch, he teases a finger along the place where the fabric meets my skin on my mound, easing it away from my body. He moves it to the side, enough to expose me to his attention and then he wastes no time. He said he wants me to come hard and come fast and he is not a liar.

His mouth covers me, tongue thrumming against my clit in a steady rhythm that is guaranteed to get me off. I spread my legs wider, inviting him in. I want this. It feels so good and my need is like a live animal inside me, clawing its way to the place where pleasure is so sweet it's almost painful.

Just when I'm about to beg him for something that I don't even know I need, he inserts two fingers deep inside me. Stroking me, filling me up only enough to make me crave something bigger, harder. I bear down on him, opening myself to his mouth and digits. I am right there. On the edge.

I'm right *there.*

It's always like the Fourth of July behind my eyelids when Jonas makes me come. Blue, red, white, green streaks across the dark night sky of my brain as I fly into them and explode into shards of light and color.

It is so good.

I come down from my high with Jonas sliding up my body to wrap his arms around me and take my mouth in a kiss. His cock, hard and hot, presses against my belly as he invades me, leaving the taste of my desire on my tongue. I moan, wedging a hand in between us to wrap my fingers around him and stroke from crown to base.

His hips flex as he drives his shaft into my hand, his body telling me just how much he wants me and all I want is to give him what he just gave me. A gift. This pleasure between us is a gift.

His words on the street come back to me and I know what I want to do, the memory I want him to take with him as he finds his path in the world. Whether he lives in the light or in his eventual darkness, I can give him something that will withstand whatever his body throws at him.

I push against his chest until he backs up to the edge of the bed. He releases my mouth and even though he looks confused he falls back on the mattress when I give him a gentle shove. His confusion deepens when he sees me go to my backpack and pull out a small bag.

"What's going on Red?"

I turn back to him and toss the condom on the bed beside him. Walking slowly, I show him my tube of lipstick, remove the cap and twist the tube. I stop just in front of him and soak him in: muscled chest heaving with his labored breathing, cock lying flat against his body, the crown red and wet. He is gorgeous, edible, and I cannot wait to have my chance to taste.

I swipe the vibrant red lipstick over my lips, replace the cap and toss it to the side before answering him.

"I thought we'd test your theory on how good this will look wrapped around the base of your cock."

CHAPTER SIX

Jonas

Holy shit. She's going to kill me.

I can't move, her words pinning me in place as my dick gets impossibly harder. On auto-pilot, I reach and take myself in hand, the slow stroke enough to calm me down a little bit.

"Red. I wasn't kidding when I said it was going to be hard and fast. I don't know if you want to play with fire tonight."

She inserts her thumbs into the sides of her panties and before I can blink they are on the floor and she's crawling onto the bed and towards me. I scoot back, it's involuntary, my body reacting to the overload of endorphins and my brain's disbelief that this is really happening. I've dreamed of this, woken up hard and aching for her and now she's here. I barely resist the urge to pinch myself.

"I'm not afraid of getting burned," she answers. "Not anymore."

I check her out, loving the confidence on her face, the spark in her eyes that says she might finally understand how amazing she is. I lean back on the pillows, releasing my cock, inviting her to come and take whatever she needs.

"I'm all yours, Red."

She laughs, easing across the bed until she can lean down and take me into her mouth with one long swallow. I buck up, digging my fingers into the coverlet. I expected her to ease into it and the immediate white hot heat of her mouth is almost enough to make me come on the spot.

Leighton hums around my length, clearly amused by my reaction and I barely bite back the curse right on the tip of my tongue. She eases herself back up and I am mesmerized by the sight of my erection sliding between her ruby red lips. The fantasy was hot but the real thing threatens to blow my mind.

"Fuck, Red. You're perfect." I swallow. "I was right. You look so good."

Her only answer is to take me inside her once again and to begin a slow and steady glide in and out of her mouth. Each pass makes me crazier until I white-knuckle grip the sheets because I don't trust myself to touch her and not hurt her at this point. I need to come. I need to find some relief from this torment.

She raises off and presses her tongue against the supersensitive spot under the head and I have to stop this insanity before I lose it. I reach down and lift her off me and throw her on her back in the middle of the bed. Her eyes are huge, lips swollen with her lipstick smudged around the edges and it is seriously the sexiest thing I've ever seen.

"I need to be inside you now," I say, more of a statement than a request but she nods in agreement anyway.

I grab the condom from the bed, rip off the foil and put it on with surprisingly steady hands. I move over her, settling between her legs and moving upwards until I can kiss her. She is so sweet and I can't get enough, sweeping my tongue in over and over again. Her hands stroke along my back, my shoulders and into my hair and I arch into her touch. I can't get enough, can't feel enough.

I pull back, locking eyes with her as I push myself inside her. She's tight, so hot and I have to struggle to keep my eyes open. Perfection is the only word I can think of and it isn't nearly enough. I move in and out slowly, easing into her body until I am buried deep inside her and nothing but air can get between us. The way it should be.

"You and me Red. Together. Okay?"

She nods her assent and I begin the in and out glide that will take us to the edge and over. I surprise myself by starting slowly, enjoying every clutch and drag of her muscle against my length. She undulates her hips against mine and I can tell by the gasps and shudders that our alignment is hitting all the right places for her over and over again.

I speed up, the prickle of sharp electricity in my lower back tantalizing and promising the prize. She opens her legs wider, raising them until her heels are resting against my ass and digging in with every upward thrust of her body. Leighton is never a passive participant in sex. She demands her pleasure, using her body to tell when to move, which way to swivel the hips. I follow her clues and I'm rewarded with a deep moan at each thrust and a fluttering of her eyelids at impact.

Somehow we maintain eye contact, the connection making everything that much more intense. I lift myself so that I can grasp her thigh, holding her in place as I snap my hips in shorter and shorter strokes. She begins talking and I lose my mind.

"Yes Jonas. You're going to make me come."

I reach down and rub her clit with my finger at the same time she starts playing with her nipples and all I can do is pray that she comes first because I'm so close the blood is roaring in my ears.

"Red, please." I'm not above begging because I need this like I need air. There is nothing to be embarrassed about when you're lucky enough to feel even a tenth of what is going on between us.

Leighton's body bows upwards, stiff and shaking as her orgasm hits her and I watch her as long as I can before mine barrels down on top of me like a tidal wave.

Fuck it feels amazing and I ride it out through every shivery pulse and then try to coax it out a little longer with shallow pumps into her body. I half-collapse on top of her as we try to catch our breath. The air in the room is slightly chilly but we burn like a furnace which is good because I don't have the energy to drag the covers over us right now.

Leighton rolls into me, tucking her head underneath my

chin and wrapping her arm around my waist. I play with her hair, twisting it around my fingers as we drift in and out. Being here with the snow raging outside and cocooned in this room feels right. The two of us against the world. I will take this with me when I leave, pull it out for the time when it gets too much.

Her next question makes me wonder if she can read my mind. "Will you paint us? Capture how we are together?"

I already have. Ten to fifteen canvases and countless sketchpad pages filled with every moment with Leighton. The dark rose of her nipples, the auburn tint of her bush. The way her eyes close when she comes.

"Yes. I will." I shift to look down at her. "Is that okay?"

"Send one to me. I want to see us."

I nod and tuck her head back under my chin, trying to slow down the rapid beat of my heart. I'll send it to her because she asked but I can't deny the panic at the thought. When she sees it everything will be out on the table between us and I'll have nowhere to hide. Because anyone who looks at a painting of Leighton will know just how much I love her.

CHAPTER SEVEN

Jonas

You can move, Red."

I should have told her ages ago but it's been a riot watching her try to lie still while I sketch. To be such a quiet person, she is a fidgeter of epic proportions. I thought she was going to squirm right off the bed at one point. Apparently I'm not doing a great job hiding my amusement because she takes one look at my face and launches a pillow at me. I dodge it, batting it back at her one-handed.

And then it's on.

Leighton launches at me with the pillow and tries to take me down but what she brings to the table in enthusiasm is no match for my larger size. But I'm a guy so I like the way her body moves against me and I let her think she's going to win for a little bit longer than is realistic.

It ends with her pinned under me, one of my legs lying on top of hers and immobilizing her. She is flushed and breathing heavily, her hair a wild mess of curls around her face. She is stunning.

"Do you give up?" I ask, panting a little myself from the exertion. She shoves against me feebly one last time and then dissolves into a frustrated groan and giggle that makes my dick pulse with expectation. I love her laugh. Everything about this girl turns me on. I run my fingers over her stomach, threatening to tickle her if she doesn't surrender. "Is that a yes?"

"Yes. Yes."

She pushes my hand away and we shift our bodies around on the bed. We end up with my head on her belly and her lying on her back with her legs extended up, feet resting on the headboard. Leighton runs her fingers through my hair and I'm in heaven.

Quiet settles over us as we watch the snow fall outside the window. The flakes are big and fat now, signs that the storm is winding down and we might catch a flight out of here tomorrow. The hint of disappointment at leaving is new but not surprising and tempers my itch to get to Rome and beyond.

"Can I see the picture?" Leighton asks, gesturing towards my sketchpad, which ended up at the end of the bed during our pillow fight.

I lift up and snag the book, handing it over to her before I can change my mind. She's seen my work before just not any of the pictures of her. I hold my breath and turn back to the window as she flips through the pages. She is focused, occasionally letting out a murmur of appreciation or recognition at the subject matter.

"I want this one." She holds up one of Landon facedown on the couch, mouth hanging open after a night of partying. The best part is his pants halfway down his legs and his smiley face boxer shorts on display. I remember that moment, he was so trashed and I was hungover but I couldn't pass up the opportunity to get the moment down on paper. "I'll frame it and give it to my mom for Christmas."

"It's yours," I say, laughing at Mrs. Greer's probable reaction. "I might have to accept your annual invite to hang out with you guys over the holidays just to see that."

"You take the photo at the moment of opening and I'll make sure to have her Xanax close by."

"It's a date," I say and then realize that I don't know where I'll be at Christmas. I haven't thought that far ahead.

"Jonas, look at me," she says and I turn to look at her. She's stopped on a sketch of her from earlier tonight. She was dozing, hand tucked against her cheek as she curled up in the covers. It was a quick rendering, a reminder for a painting I would execute later. She riffles through the pages and finds some other sketches of her, playing the violin and sitting on the couch in my apartment, her brother by her side. "Is this how you see me?"

"You don't?"

She cuts me a look that warns me that she's not going to let me fuck around with the question. "I want to know how *you* see me."

I pause, trying to figure out what she's really asking.

"Don't think about it. Just tell me."

And then I know what this is about and I'm happy to tell her.

"Yeah, I do. I see you exactly like that." I reach up and snag her hand, weaving our fingers together. "You can sleep like that because you know who you are and you're comfortable in your skin. You have a gift that allows you to make music that touches people. You give it so freely, so openly, they just can't help but respond to you. I think you're the bravest person I know."

"I'm not brave," she whispers, her head dipping forward as she tries to hide behind the fall of her hair. I release her hand and push the strands back behind her ear, letting my touch linger over the soft skin of her cheek.

"You are." I laugh. "Look at you going on your first trip to Ireland and taking a job that will take you all over the fucking world. I know it freaks you out but you're doing it anyway. I'd say that's pretty brave."

She nods, swallowing hard and chuckling a little bit. "My parents think I'm biting off more than I can chew."

"They just worry about you. It's in their job description to lie awake at night and get an ulcer fixating on things that will never happen."

"I know and I understand why. I was really sick and they were terrified that they were going to lose me and then they worried that Landon would get sick too."

I hadn't thought about that before. Mr. and Mrs. Greer

must have been insane wondering if their son would get cancer as well. It's not such a leap when you consider they are twins. It must have been a nightmare.

"What was it like being sick?" I've never asked her before but suddenly I feel like she might be one of the few people who might get what is going on in my head.

"The worst part about it is worrying about how it impacts other people," she says. "At first I was worried that I would die but I got over it when my life became nothing but appointments and needles and my hair falling out. The worst part was the fear in my mom's eyes and trying to hide it when I was knocked on my ass by something. She'd get this look, a thousand yard stare. I hated it because I knew she was trying to hide from all of the terrifying shit going through her head."

"I know that look. My mom had it when I got my diagnosis." It sucked and I felt a little guilty for putting her through this even though it isn't because of anything I did. "I always make sure I keep it upbeat around her because I don't want her worrying more than she already is. If I'm cool about it then she can handle it better."

"Exactly," she agrees, nodding as she places the pad on the bed and begins that amazing sift of fingers through my hair again. "The treatments, being tired all the time, the constant doctors gave me clear focus. I just wanted to get through the next phase and I took each day and every little victory like I'd won a gold medal at the Olympics. One foot in front of the other."

"And now?"

"I'm just tired of living under the weight of the words 'remission' and 'cancer survivor'." She stops the caress of my head to clarify. "I'm glad I got better and beat it, don't get me wrong, but I'm ready to find out who I am beyond those labels."

"I think that's good." I pause and then nudge her with a poke to her side that makes her giggle and squirm away. "I'd say that's pretty brave, Red."

She makes a face at me and tugs on my hair. I swat her

hands away but relax into her touch again when she resumes stroking my scalp. It's late and I think we should probably go to sleep but I can't move. The quiet, her hands in my hair and her soft naked body against mine is pretty damn perfect.

"Jonas?" she asks.

"Yeah?"

"Are you afraid?"

I stop breathing. My skin crawls with awareness as I weigh my options of fight or flight. I don't want to argue with her, she's only asking because she cares about me. And I don't want to run either—not from Leighton. This night is flying by and I want to wring out every moment I have with her. It's been an escape, a respite from the reality of what is coming. But her question brings it all crashing down and plants it right in the middle of the bed with us.

She takes my silence as anger and quickly backtracks. "Forget it. I shouldn't have—"

"Yes. I'm afraid," I blurt out because I don't want her to feel like she can't ask me, like we aren't close enough. I didn't hesitate to tell her about the diagnosis and I know I can trust her with this part of it too. "I'm fucking terrified."

She murmurs something low but unintelligible but I don't need to know the words to understand the feeling. Her lips brushing against my forehead is almost too much and I reach up to grab her, holding her close and wrapping my arms around her neck.

"I know in my head that this is manageable and that I can have a full life. Fuck, I might have most of my life with mostly normal vision before I'm unable to see." And here is where I get down to it and bare it all. "But my Grandpa was forty-three and the thing pinging loudly in my head is that it is only twenty years from now and twenty years doesn't feel so goddamn long."

"So the traveling "

"I'm terrified that I'm not going to see all I can see before it's nothing but blackness." I ball my hands into fists and press them against my eyes, unable to stop the shaking that has now taken over my body. Fear and anger is a very powerful combination and I'm suspended between the two. "Even if I get my twenty years I think of all the shit I'm going to miss. Forget all the Hallmark card bullshit about cherishing a sunset, I'm going to miss seeing my parents as they age, my own kids and wife. They'll all be perpetually whatever age they are when I lose my sight. I might never see my grandkids." I grit my teeth and spit out the rest of my venom and wait for her reaction. "So yes, I'm afraid but I'm also fucking angry at this shitty hand I've been dealt."

"I can't stand the thought of you being alone somewhere in the world and working through this on your own," she whispers against my cheek, her fingers resuming their soothing pattern in my hair. "Can't you come back? Stay with me. Finish school and let me—"

I cut her off because this is the place where we cannot go. *I* cannot go. How can I ask her take on a future with a man who will one day be blind and dependent? She can have anyone she wants, someone who will be whole and I can't tie her down to me. I grab her hand and stop her movement, looking at her until she lifts her gaze to mine.

"Leighton, don't ask me this. Just don't." I give her hand a squeeze, letting her know that I am serious about this point. "I have to go and find my way on this and I can't ask you to do it with me."

"What if I want to do this?"

"It doesn't matter." I soften my tone when the hurt flares in her eyes. The last thing I want to do is hurt her, but lying would only lead to pain for her in the long run. "I am barely hanging on right now and I don't know where I'm going or where I'm going to end up. You've caught me on a good day or you're the reason it's been a good day but I'm not a person you want to be around right now. I need to work through this and I can't do it if I'm worried about how you are handling all of it. I'll slip into a black mood and lash out and you will be hurt."

"You wouldn't hurt me."

"Yes, I will." I cup her jaw, running my thumb along the plump swell of her bottom lip. I lean up and kiss her, lingering over it with a gentle brush of my flesh on hers. "You have a wonderful opportunity ahead of you and you need to just go and do it. I can't saddle you with a future that I'm not even sure of at this point. Just forget me Leighton."

"You're asking the impossible," she says with a stubborn steel in her voice.

"Well then, you just need to let me go."

CHAPTER EIGHT

Leighton

I wake up with Jonas between my legs, tongue sliding along my clit in slow, easy strokes.

The covers are thrown off the bed and my overheated skin is exposed to the chill of the air in the room. I shift as a pulse of pleasure ripples through my body, a moan escaping into the silence. It's loud and long and alerts him that I'm fully awake.

He raises his head, lips slick, eyes dark with lust but his grin is all Jonas. "You sleep like the dead."

"And you're trying to kill me." The last two words stutter as he trails a hand across my body and captures a nipple with his fingers. A lazy swirl, the slightest tug and I'm thrusting my sex towards him, begging him to put his mouth back on me. "Jonas, please."

"Red. You should never have to beg," he whispers and lowers his head back to me and delivers his carnal kiss.

I am a mess. Hot. Cold. Shivery all over. Just on the edge of flying apart. I don't know how long he's been going down on me but I'm ready to shatter into a million pieces.

His tongue zeroes in on my clit. He's wasting no time to get me off. Not teasing. It's like he wants me to fall apart at Mach 1 and I'm ready to oblige.

It begins deep inside me, a flash and tingle in my belly and the next thing I know, I'm on fire and it is the most delicious burn. Instead of running from it, I reach for it and try to hold on as long as I can.

Jonas rises from between my legs, a sleepy but intensely feral look on his face as he lifts me up and dives in for a deep, possessive kiss. Our tongues spar for dominance and I wrap my arms around his neck as I crawl into his lap. His hands roam everywhere, my back, my shoulders, and my ass where he ends his exploration with a squeeze.

This embrace is intense and suddenly all of the playfulness from earlier is gone. This is it. Our last few hours together. We'll get on separate planes and I don't know when I'll see him again. I clasp his face in my hands and pour everything into my kiss. I can't tell him what's going on in my head. I know what he needs to do to be at peace and I can't take that from him.

My body won't lie though and I can only hope that he doesn't fully understand its language.

His erection is hard and demanding between us and I grind into it, my own arousal spiking again with the memory of how good he feels inside me. It is the only thing that will soothe the ache in my chest.

I break the kiss and we are both breathless.

"I need you," he whispers, voice soft with tenderness that makes my chest ache and expand to the point where my whole body hurts with the want of it.

"I need you too." I get another condom out of my bag and hand it to him and watch as he slides it down over his length.

He remains seated on the side of the bed and I move to straddle him. I loop my arms around his neck, watching his face as he slowly enters me. He is big, hard and I'm tender from last night. It's almost too much but I wait, letting out a sigh when my body melts around him.

He groans, no doubt feeling the moment I let all my guard down and welcome him inside. He's so deep. Not just in the physical sense but inside *me*—inside my soul. Inside my heart.

I lean down and kiss him softly and it's the signal he needs to begin the slow glide, the intimate push and pull. I lift myself up and let gravity pull me down, relishing every stretch as I strive for the climax that is right there already. I want him so much. I need him so much.

"Leighton," he breathes against my neck, his face buried in my hair.

I hang on tight, closing my eyes and memorizing every sound, every scent. I don't want it to end but with his next thrust I am falling. Coming. Melting.

"Yes. Give it all to me," he murmurs and then he is still beneath me as his orgasm hits. He tightens his arms around me as if he wants to absorb me into his body. I hang onto him not loosening my grip until he relaxes.

We stay like that, wrapped around each other for what seems like forever but it is still over too soon. My eyes burn, tears scalding me as I struggle to keep them in. I'm breaking apart inside and I just know I will fly apart when he lets me go.

I am strong. He is strong. I know we can do this but I don't want to. We shouldn't have to.

"Jonas. Don't go to Rome. Go to Dublin with me and then come back to school. Don't end us before we have a chance to begin. Let me be there for you, no matter what happens."

The words are out of my mouth before I realize what I've said but the utter stillness of his body against mine tells me that he heard every word. When he does move it is precise, careful motions that unwind us from each other. He stands beside the bed but will not look at me. I open my mouth to take it back, to apologize. I may argue with him. It is completely moot when he beats me to it.

"I asked you not to do this." He walks towards the bathroom, stopping just inside the door and delivers his final verdict before going inside and shutting me out. "All this does is break both of our hearts."

I hold back the tears until I hear the shower running.

CHAPTER NINE

Jonas

I might be making the biggest mistake of my life but I'm going to do it anyway.

The rest of the morning after my exit into the shower had been strained. Leighton was hurt and maybe embarrassed and I was angry at the whole damn situation. She didn't look at me with eyes that condemned me for last night, her expression was much worse. She was unhappy.

Everything about her screamed out her broken emotions but she put on a brave face and tried to act like nothing was wrong. She made small talk which made my teeth ache, laughed and chatted with the staff at the hotel and trudged through the snow with no complaint as we tried to make our new flights.

The snow had stopped and the sun was bright in a sky so blue it looked like I painted it. The airport was open and ready for business and we were in the terminal ready to head to our separate gates. Leighton was anxious, the tight grip of her hand on her backpack and the strap of Wonder Woman's case noticeable. She was ready to ditch me as soon as she could and I'd be lying if I said it didn't kill me to let her do it.

"Thank you for rescuing me from a night spent on the floor," she says, refusing to meet my gaze. "I better go."

"Red, wait." I grab her arm as she turns away, stopping her progress when I wrap my arms around her and hold her close to me. She's stiff as a board and no matter how much I try to soothe her, she's unresponsive. "Leighton—"

"Please let go of me Jonas." Her voice is low and almost lost in the various noises in the terminal but I catch the words and her underlying tone of heartbreak. Fuck, I know it. I feel it too but there are so many reasons that we don't work right now and may never work. So why can't I let her go?

"Leighton."

"Let me go Jonas."

I hear the decision in her voice and feel the resolve in her bones. She is doing as I asked and the one thing I can do is not make it harder than it already is. I release her, memorizing everything from the smell of the hotel shampoo in her hair to the coffee she drank before we ventured out into the cold.

"Have a good flight Jonas and please let Landon know where you are and that you're okay." She meets my eyes for the briefest second before it skitters away and she turns towards her gate.

I watch her go, only sheer determination turning my body in the opposite direction towards my own departure gate. I weave in and out of the people, dodging rolling suitcases and sleepy kids as I settle in to wait. My flight boards in a little over an hour so I find an empty seat facing the large expanse of windows and the planes all lined up outside.

Snow is plowed and pushed to the sides in huge mounds dirtied by all the grit and grime from the airport runway. Men and women scramble outside in the cold to load luggage and inspect the planes. It's normally a scene I would sketch, the wealth of different faces and body types almost irresistible, but today I don't want to pull out the pad and flip past the pages of Leighton. I just can't.

I decide to make a necessary call and I pull out my phone, hitting speed dial for Landon. The phone rings on his end a few times before he picks it up with a sleepy, "Hello".

"Hey Landon. It's me."

"Jonas!" He perks up on the other end and I can hear his bed sheets rustling over the line. "So did you and Leighton survive the blizzard?"

I want to tell him that I barely made it out alive but I stick to the facts. "She's fine and headed to her gate. Her flight leaves at 1:20. Same flight number as yesterday." I relay the facts I know he'll pass on to his mom and prepare to get off the phone. I'm not really in the mood to talk.

Landon apparently is up and ready to chat.

"So, last night was okay? I really appreciate you looking after her. My mom was driving me nuts."

"It was fine. We had a decent room and went to a pub and grabbed a bite to eat. It worked out great." I hesitate and then add. "I told her about my diagnosis."

He whistles, long and low on his side of the phone and I hear him move as he sits up in his bed. I'm kind of anxious to see what Landon thinks about this whole thing. He's my best friend and he's wicked smart but he's Leighton's brother and I can't imagine he's going to be happy about what happened.

"How'd she take the news?"

"She was cool. It upset her but she was a rock."

"Well, that's my sister. She's got a backbone of steel."

I pull back the phone and stare at it. Who is this guy? "What? What about her being fragile?"

"Buddy, that was four years ago when I was an asshole and seeing everything through the lens of my parents. Growing up in a house where a kid had cancer is different and all I remembered was the tubes and drugs and my sister lying in a bed barely hanging on. It fucks you up."

"We talked about it." I remembered what she said and how she'd carried all of the weight of it on her very young shoulders. "Her illness, we talked about it."

"My parents were great and strong and did everything you are supposed to do but she was the one who carried all of us. Don't get me wrong, she had her moments where the shit hit the fan and she fell apart but her attitude and the way she faced it head on set the tone for the rest of the family. I didn't get it until later." He laughed. "My sister is *anything* but fragile."

Oh Jesus. I scrub my hand over my face and try to wipe away the confusion. I have no idea what he's trying to tell me.

"Landon, spit it out."

"Fine Jonas, here it is. I know that you guys have had something going on since I caught you with your tongue down her throat freshman year."

I open my mouth to protest but he's right. Not much to argue about there.

He continues. "And I know she spent the night with you on New Year's Eve."

"How?"

"I'm not blind. You guys have been doing the 'I slept with you and it rocked my world but I'm going to avoid you' dance for the last two months. It's exhausting."

Well, shit.

"And I'm not saying that you've got to marry her or anything but the two of you are good together and she can't do any worse than Brian-the-shitface."

"Well, thanks for the endorsement."

"I know you better than anyone else and although you can be a douche, you're honest and a good guy." He laughed to himself. "And it's really none of my fucking business but since you asked "

"I didn't."

"Yes. You did." He cuts me off before I can protest any more. "I get that you need to see the world before you lose your vision and I think you should. It's a shitty thing that's happened to you and I don't blame you at all for doing what you need to do."

"But?"

"But you need to come back and graduate and figure this shit out with Leighton and then make your plans to see the world and paint every fucking sunset on the planet." He huffs out a laugh of sorts and I can picture him in my mind, pushing his glasses up on his nose and making his hair stand up all over his head like an electrocuted Einstein. "Fuck Jonas, even Mother Nature was telling the two of you to get your shit together and figure it out."

"You're telling me that the Universe made this blizzard to force Leighton and I together?" I shake my head even though he can't see it. "That's not very logical Mr.-Math-Major."

"This isn't about numbers. It's about the heart and *I'm* smart enough to know the difference."

That shuts me up. I take a few moments to process all these pearls of wisdom and he waits patiently as I figure out what feels like my whole future.

"I don't have any idea what is going to happen. No idea how I'm going to handle the changes or anything."

"Well if you did I'd tell you to go buy some lottery tickets for me because the thought of graduating and living on a starting salary for a math teacher is starting to give me the shakes." We both laugh and then when we quiet down he adds, "Nobody can guarantee anything. Her cancer might come back or my turn might be next. You could get hit by a bus in Rome. Nothing is guaranteed except that it will be shitty at times but I think she's strong enough to handle it."

I freeze. It's exactly what Gabe said last night. I then realize that I've done exactly what her family did—underestimated Leighton. She is strong enough to handle it. Not that she won't have challenges or be scared for me but she can push on through.

And I need her.

I don't know if I'm strong enough to get through it all. I just know I have a better shot at it if Leighton is with me.

And I still want to see the world, store up the memories but I want her to be part of that. I can't imagine looking back and not seeing Leighton in the movie reel of my life in a starring role.

"I've got to go," I say into the phone, grabbing my backpack and looking for the closest ticket counter. I don't have much time if I'm going to fix this.

"Yeah. You do." Landon laughs into the phone. "Have a pint for me in Dublin and tell my sister to call mom."

CHAPTER TEN

Leighton

I keep telling myself that this is the right way to end things.

Quick. Just like pulling off a Band-Aid. And I will be spared the shit-tastic, "Groundhog Day" version of seeing Jonas all over campus. With Landon. In the student quad. With other women. Nope, he'll be in Rome and then anywhere else the wind will take him and I'll strain a muscle listening for any clue from my brother about where Jonas is and how he is doing.

It will not be enough. It is not enough.

I want to be with him. Asking him was easy once I'd started, the words falling out of my mouth like the notes singing out from my instrument. It was like breathing. Wanting him is part of me. My DNA has shifted to incorporate him into my cellular structure, my soul. To not ask him would have caused me physical pain.

But his rejection hurts like a bitch too. I understand his reason, I really do. I can't imagine what he is going through and what he is feeling. I just want to be with him. To help him. To love him.

He needs space to figure stuff out in his head without having to worry about me and how I'm handling it. I might be the one person in his life, besides Grandpa Sutton, who gets it. I remember the burden of worrying about my parents and Landon when I was sick. You have no control over your body but you still feel like you'll let them down if you don't get better.

The last thing I want to do is be a burden for Jonas.

I shove the stupid airline magazine into the pocket on the back of the seat in front of me, smiling in apology when the person occupying it turns around with a glare. Apparently I was trying to shove my heartbreak into the pocket along with it.

I shift in the seat, itching to pull out Wonder Woman and soothe myself by playing her for a while but I can't. This is going to be a long flight.

The flight attendant who greeted me at the door enters the coach section of the cabin with purpose and stops at my row. She is still smiling, every hair in place and nails buffed to a high sheen but it's the weird gleam in her eyes that has me wondering if I'm headed for a cavity search.

"Leighton Greer?" she asks in greeting, using that vocal uplift at the end of it to indicate a question.

"Yes? Is something wrong?"

"No. Not all," she replies, glancing up into the open overhead compartment and then back to me. "I just need you to gather your things and come with me."

"What? Why?" Panic rises in my gut as I contemplate the possibility that I might actually be headed to a meeting with a woman with a latex glove and K-Y jelly inside the terminal. "Is there something wrong?"

She laughs because it's not *her ass* in jeopardy and my irritation spikes a little higher.

"No. You are fine. You've been upgraded to first class for your flight."

I get up out of my seat on auto-pilot when she reaches up and pulls my violin out of the bin and hands it to me. I'm following her lead but my brain does not compute what she is saying. We walk three or four more steps down the aisle before my mouth catches up with my feet.

"Was it my mother?" It would be just like her to do it too. She'd put me in a bubble if they offered that option. I love her but we're going to have a talk about her worrying so much when I get home. Upgrades aren't cheap and while my folks aren't destitute they can't throw around money like the Kardashians.

The flight attendant ignores my question, leading me past the flimsy curtain that separates the two parts of the cabin. She stops in front of one of the double-wide, comfortable leather seats and points to an empty spot.

"Here's your seat." She takes Wonder Woman out of my hands and smiles. "I'll store this up front for you and be back in a few moments to get your drink order. Have a great flight."

She turns without any further explanation and I stare after her, still unsure about what is happening here. I edge forward to sit down and finally notice the person occupying the window seat next to mine.

When he turns and smiles up at me my legs give out and I land in the seat in a heap, mouth hanging open.

Jonas grins even wider and leans forward to whisper in my ear, "Hey Red."

***

Jonas

I'm not sure if she's going to hit me or kiss me so I make a command decision.

I lift my hand, ignoring the way it shakes, and slide it along her jaw until I can cup the back of her neck. I tug lightly, she resists for a moment and panic spikes my body temperature. I look up quickly to make eye contact, expecting to see a fight but what I get is an open vulnerable longing that tells me that this was the best decision I ever made.

I kiss her. I need to taste her, to experience her surrender and acceptance as she opens to my request. I need it because I am completely, utterly, totally hers and I can't stand the idea of swinging out here alone without her there to catch me.

I break off the kiss, only taking a moment to push up the armrest divider and then I grab her and haul her into my lap. The lady behind us murmurs a startled "oh my" but I ignore her, choosing instead to kiss the shit out of the woman I love.

Leighton wraps her arms around my neck and gives me

as good as she gets. She's not holding back and I go along for the wild ride. I expect to be called out by the flight attendant any minute now for trying to join the mile high club while still parked at the gate but I really don't care. Any U.S. Marshall would take one look at Red and wish me luck.

We finally break it off to catch our breath and I steel myself to tell her all the stuff she deserves to hear, but one thing must be done first.

"Forgive me. I'm sorry I was such a stubborn asshole and I can't promise you that I won't pull another dick move at some time in the future but I'm sorry for making you cry and for rejecting you. I'm scared and I don't know how this is going to end up for me but I don't want to push you away. In fact, I don't know how I'll get through this if I don't have you by my side. So don't make me get off this plane, please."

"What *are* you doing here?" she asks on a laugh, her fingers tracing my face like she's afraid I'll disappear. "Are you real?"

"Yeah. I'm real and not going anywhere."

"What?"

"I'm going to Dublin with you."

She shakes her head in confusion. "What? What about Rome?"

"I'll get there." I smooth a stray curl back from her face. "I'll go when you go there with the philharmonic or we can plan another trip."

"Jonas. I don't want you to miss anything. What about your paintings? The memories you want to save for later?" She tears up and even though she tries to blink them away, I see them. When one escapes and trails down her cheek I catch it with my finger and sweep it away.

"Oh, Red," I say, smiling down at her. The words come easy because I can't have her thinking for one minute that she's making me miss anything. "I don't want to paint a picture of those places without you in it. I want every memory to be of you and me, loving each other every second of our lives."

"Love?" she asks on a whisper, her eyes huge and a tremble in her voice.

"Oh yeah. I love you. So much it hurts. And more than anything, the last thing I want to see is your face. You okay with that?"

She nods. "I'm *really* okay with that."

"And you love me?" I can see it written all over her face but I want to hear the words.

"Oh yeah. I love you."

We lean in for another kiss but the flight attendant announces that we need to be in our seats to prepare for takeoff. Leighton slides off my lap and with goofy grins plastered on our faces we fasten our seatbelts and settle in for our flight. I reach over to take her hand and she leans to the side to rest against my shoulder. I hear her giggle and look down to see what's so funny.

"What are we going to tell Landon? He's going to freak."

I lean over and nuzzle her hair, pressing my lips to the soft spot just behind her ear before I whisper, "We'll tell him it started with one little kiss."

Dear Reader –

Thanks so much for reading my book. If you enjoyed this novella you can find out the latest info on my next release and enter for the monthly giveaway by signing up for my newsletter. You can also drop me a line at robin@robincovingtonromance.com. I'd love to hear from you.

And if you are so inclined, please leave a review on Amazon, Barnes & Noble, iBooks, or Goodreads.

I love to explore the theme of fooling around and falling in love in my books and I adore a hero who falls hard. When I'm not writing sexy, sizzling romance, I collect tasty man candy pics, indulge in a little comic book geek love, collect red nail polish, and obsess over Dean Winchester. Don't send chocolate . . . send eye-candy!

There are so many great books out there and I'm grateful that you spent your money and time to read my book.

Xx,
Robin

****

Social Media Links:
Website: http://www.robincovingtonromance.com/
Facebook Profile: http://on.fb.me/YSW9n3
Facebook Page: http://on.fb.me/1fCyWuQ
Twitter: @RobinCovington
Pinterest: http://www.pinterest.com/
    robincovington1/
Newsletter: http://eepurl.com/qj_cz

If you enjoyed ***ONE LITTLE KISS***, check out my other books:

A NIGHT OF SOUTHERN COMFORT
HIS SOUTHERN TEMPTATION
SWEET SOUTHERN BETRAYAL
PLAYING THE PART
SEX & THE SINGLE VAMP
PLAYING WITH THE DRUMMER
DARING THE PLAYER
TEMPTATION
SECRET SANTA BABY